The Trouble
With Diamonds

The Trouble With Diamonds

◆·◆·◆·◆·◆·◆·◆·◆·◆·◆·◆·◆·◆

SCOTT CORBETT

illustrated by Bert Dodson

E. P. DUTTON   NEW YORK

The text of this book is a considerably revised version
of *Diamonds Are Trouble* by Scott Corbett, published in
1967 by Holt, Rinehart and Winston.

Text copyright © 1967, 1985 by Scott Corbett
Illustrations copyright © 1985 by Bert Dodson

Library of Congress Cataloging in Publication Data

Corbett, Scott.
    The trouble with diamonds.

    Rev. ed. of: Diamonds are trouble. 1st ed. 1967.
    Summary: After Jeff Adams gets a summer job at a country inn,
his first duty is to help the owner trap a suspected jewel thief.
    1. Children's stories, American. [1. Mystery and detective
stories.   2. Summer employment—Fiction]   I. Corbett, Scott.
Diamonds are trouble.   II. Dodson, Bert, ill.   III. Title.
PZ7.C79938TS   1985   [Fic]   84-18762
ISBN 0-525-44190-5

Published in the United States by E. P. Dutton, Inc.,
2 Park Avenue, New York, N.Y. 10016

Published simultaneously in Canada by
Fitzhenry & Whiteside Limited, Toronto

Editor: Julie Amper   Designer: Edith T. Weinberg

Printed in the U.S.A.   COBE   Revised Edition

10 9 8 7 6 5 4 3 2 1

to Bill Arbuckle,
who reminds me of Ambrose Bunker

1

The sign beside the gravel driveway said:

WESTHAM INN
Ambrose Bunker, Prop.

This was the place. Ahead of him, the driveway curved off into pitch darkness. Jeff Adams picked his way along the white gravel for a few yards, then stopped. One of his sneakers' shoelaces was dragging. He stepped off beside a bush, put down his bag, and stooped to tie the lace.

On the other side of the driveway, not far ahead, he could see some small dark buildings—cottages, probably. Suddenly something else caught his eye. Something moving. Something had slipped across the driveway. A man. The man came nearer, tiptoeing along like someone up to no good. He stopped alongside the nearest cottage and went to work on one of the window screens.

Slowly he managed to push it up in its slot.

Jeff was a peaceable soul who didn't go around looking for trouble. At the same time, he was a lot stronger than his gangly string-bean body made him look, and here was Opportunity!

How to nail down a summer job at the inn: Catch a burglar!

Staying off the gravel, he crept forward. The man was just getting ready to climb through the window when Jeff pounced on him.

There was a brief wrestling match. Then Jeff was sitting like a stork on top of a short, plump, bald man who stared up at him popeyed through round glasses. Sitting on him was like sitting on a small round hill. The burglar had not been dieting lately. Jeff pinned his arms against the ground and tried to sound really nasty.

"All right, fellah, now let's go see Mr. Bunker!"

"What do you mean?" snapped the man. "I *am* Mr. Bunker!"

Jeff gaped down at him. Ambrose Bunker snorted.

"Oh, boy! Something tells me you're that kid who called about a summer job!"

"Yes, sir! Jeff Adams!"

"I didn't expect you till tomorrow!"

"Oh! Gee, I thought you said—"

"Never mind what you thought! Do you usually ask someone for a job while you're sitting on his stomach?"

"Oh, no, sir!" Jeff leaped off the small round hill like a grasshopper. Mr. Bunker rose and brushed himself off angrily. And Jeff made things worse by snickering. He couldn't help it.

"I'll admit, this is an unusual job interview, sir."

"Hah! The last thing I need around here is a wise guy who jumps me in the dark!"

It sounded as if the job was slipping away from him. Desperate measures were called for—a little blackmail, maybe? Jeff glanced at the open window.

"Oh, I don't know about that. . . ."

The small plump man's round eyes followed his glance.

"Hey!" Ambrose Bunker drew himself up, which still left him a foot shorter than Jeff. "Now, wait a minute! It's not the way you think!"

"I was only fooling, sir. But what I can't figure out is why you didn't just take an extra key for this cottage and—"

"I lost it! Listen, kid, you just come up to the inn, and I'll explain everything. Wait till I pull this screen down. . . ."

"I'll get my bag."

Jeff hurried down the driveway, trying not to laugh. His job prospects were looking better and better!

4

2

◇•◇•◇•◇•◇•◇•◇•◇•◇•◇•◇

The inn sat sideways to the drive. Mr. Bunker was waiting for him at a back entrance. He was wiping his bald head with his handkerchief. He frowned at Jeff.

"What a workout! It's all I can do to get my breath back!"

The inn was a pleasant, rambling old house that dated from colonial times. It was painted barn red. It was not large, maybe fifteen rooms. Jeff followed Mr. Bunker inside.

Nobody else seemed to be around. They had entered a cozy lounge made for sociability, with well-cushioned wooden chairs around small tables and a small bar in one corner. The ceiling beams were only a few inches above Jeff's head.

"Coffee?" barked Mr. Bunker.

"Yes, sir!"

"Come and get it."

The innkeeper walked through a doorway into the kitchen. Jeff followed.

Bonk!

"What was that?" he cried, looking around nervously.

"My head, sir."

"Better learn to duck—if you stay, that is."

When Jeff's head had cleared, he looked around the kitchen. A coffeepot was sitting on the big electric stove.

"Grab a couple of cups over there."

Jeff took cups and saucers from a shelf and brought them to the stove. He knew he was being watched, and why. The innkeeper observed the quick, efficient way he moved—except for the tendency to bump his head, Jeff was not awkward. Remembering to duck this time, he carried the cups in to a round table without slopping any coffee into the saucers. They sat down.

"You a basketball player?"

"No, sir. I've got the height but not the talent, so I'll have to get to college on my own. That's why I need a summer job."

"I see. Where's home?"

Jeff felt a little stab of homesickness as he mentioned a small town in Vermont.

"So. A country boy, eh?"

"Yes, sir, but I'm willing to learn sophisticated ways," said Jeff with a grin. "Besides, like I said on the phone, I worked last summer at an inn in New Hampshire, so I know a little bit about it."

"Why didn't you get a job there this summer?"

"I couldn't. They went broke."

"Humph! With you around, maybe I'll go broke, too. Well, anyway, that's your story, is it?"

"Yes, sir, that's my story," said Jeff solemnly. "Now how about yours?"

Mr. Bunker gave him a hard look, but his lips twitched.

"Well, I'll go straight to the point. My problem is Mrs. Myra Walling! My best customer. We're old friends. She spends part of the summer here every year. She comes early, before the real season begins, when it's nice to have some customers. She's amusing, she's rich, she's generous, she's good company. But this year she's driving me crazy!"

"Why is that, sir?"

"She brought Sparkles!"

Jeff visualized a fluffy lapdog with beady sparkling eyes, a nasty little bark, and sharp teeth.

"Sparkles?"

"Sparkles is her nickname for a diamond necklace, the likes of which you've never seen outside the movies. The stones in it are the size of hens' eggs—jumbos! I can hardly sleep nights, worrying about

someone stealing it. And now, to make things worse, this guy Wolfe shows up."

"Who's he?"

"That's exactly what I'd like to know. A few days ago, Mr. Augustus V. Wolfe checked in. Big, smooth fat man dressed in expensive, well-tailored clothes, driving a flashy sedan, which I could tell was a rental. He took a cottage for two weeks! That's nice business to have this early. I should have been pleased, but I wasn't. Why did he show up here now, when my only other guest is a wealthy woman with a priceless necklace?"

Mr. Bunker leaned back and put his fingers together into a steeple. His eyes narrowed.

"Right away he bothered me. I knew I was onto something. I didn't like the way he looked at Sparkles. Like it gave him itchy palms. He said he used to be in the furniture business, but had retired. He gave a Chicago address as home. But—well, he worried me. It was time for a little private investigation."

Jeff's eyes did a little private investigation of their own and came up with an important clue. The low bookshelves that lined the room were full of paperbacks, and most of them were mysteries. And the way Mr. Bunker was sitting back with his fingers together and his eyes narrowed—well, Jeff had read a few mystery novels himself, and he could think of several detectives who did that. Jeff was willing to bet that Mr. Bunker was one of those mystery fans who are always just dying to play detective themselves—and here was his chance. He was creating a complete jewel-robbery fantasy out of thin air, besides which—

"Well, why worry, sir? Sparkles must be insured, anyway, so—"

Mr. Bunker sat bolt upright, astonished and scornful.

"What? You certainly didn't learn much at that other inn, if you think *that!* The headlines wouldn't explain that the necklace was insured; the headlines would say PRICELESS DIAMOND NECKLACE STOLEN AT WESTHAM INN—the worst kind of publicity! Besides, Myra might get hurt in the process!"

Jeff realized it was time to flatter the Great Detective.

"Gee, I never thought of that, Mr. Bunker. You're right."

Mr. Bunker looked pleased. He sat back and resumed the position—fingers together, eyes narrowed.

"Well, anyway. Mrs. Walling and Wolfe got along fine—Myra likes everybody—and tonight she took him off to a big cocktail party she'd been invited to. I had the place to myself. So first I got on the phone and dialed Information in Chicago."

Mr. Bunker paused dramatically.

"There was no Augustus V. Wolfe listed at any address in Chicago!"

Maybe an unlisted number? thought Jeff, who might be a small-town boy but who *had* worked at that other inn and had learned a few things. But since he wanted a job at *this* inn, what he said was,

"Gee! How about that!"

"Exactly. This made me even more suspicious. That was when I decided to have a look in his cottage. Maybe I could find some evidence he's a phony. He's probably too smart for that, but still, you never can tell. Even smart crooks make stupid mistakes."

I wonder which book that line came from? Jeff asked himself. Probably a hundred of them. But by now another thought had occurred to Jeff: Mr. Bunker was fun! And it would be fun to work here and see how his fantasy developed.

Meanwhile, an annoyed look crossed the innkeeper's round face.

"I should talk about mistakes, though! I swear, it's not my night. First off, I started across the side lawn in the dark—and somebody had forgotten to pull up a croquet wicket. I took an awful flop, and the extra key to Wolfe's cottage went flying out of my hand. When I got up, I couldn't find it anywhere."

Jeff pictured the scene and tried to keep a straight face. Mr. Bunker glared at him. Finally they both laughed.

"All right, Jeff! So now I was getting stubborn. I was going to have a look around in Wolfe's cottage

11

even if I had to climb in the window. I knew one of his window catches didn't work right, so . . ."

"I'll fix it tomorrow. And so then you started to climb in the window, and some punk kid jumped you."

"Exactly!"

Jeff made a quick decision. There was no question about one thing: The best way to make sure of his job was by playing along with his boss's crazy ideas. He looked at his watch.

"When will they be back?"

"Not for a long time. They're going to stop somewhere for dinner after the cocktail party."

They eyed each other silently for no more than three seconds.

"Well, then," said Jeff, "what are we waiting for?"

Mr. Bunker leaned forward.

"Young man," he said, "you just *may* have got yourself a job!"

3

◇·◇·◇·◇·◇·◇·◇·◇·◇·◇·◇·◇·◇

Jeff braced his back against the cottage wall and laced his fingers together. He had not been at West-ham Inn half an hour, yet here he was, getting ready to boost his boss through a guest's cottage window! It was not the kind of summer work he had expected to be doing.

A couple of grunts from each of them, and Mr. Bunker was through the window. Turning on a light, he went to work. Jeff stood guard outside.

The night was still and clear, but moonless—just right for dark and dirty deeds. Somewhere not far away, a dog barked. The only other sound was the purr of a car going by on the road below the inn. Now and then, Jeff glanced through the window to see how Mr. Bunker was doing and smiled when he saw how serious the plump man was. If he wanted to imitate his favorite private eye, why not? Maybe this would help him get it out of his system, especially if he didn't find anything suspicious.

A loud snuffle behind him and a hard bump against Jeff's leg made him jump.

"Yi!"

Mr. Bunker rushed to the window.

"What—what—?"

"Something— Oh! It's a dog! A big bulldog!"

"Ruby!" cried Mr. Bunker. "Sit!"

But Ruby was already sitting, wagging her flimsy excuse of a tail and panting mildly as she looked up at Jeff.

"Gee! I'm lucky she didn't take my leg off!"

"That creampuff? She wouldn't take a leg off a cricket!" Her master stuck his head out the window. "Ruby, beat it! We don't need you here!"

Ruby gave Jeff a humorous look and ambled off into the dark. Mr. Bunker went back to work. He opened a suitcase. Jeff passed the time by looking around at the grounds. The drive went past three other cottages, then circled in front of the inn. On the other side of the drive was a parking area. Jeff checked on his boss again and saw he had stopped to look at something.

"Find something, sir?"

"Well, maybe . . ."

Then Jeff heard the purr of another car. He turned to listen.

"Uh-oh."

No question about it. This one was slowing down. He whirled back to the window.

"Lights out! Car coming!"

Mr. Bunker gasped, then leaped to the wall switch, and snapped off the light. Blackness.

"Whoever it is, keep them away from here! I've got to close this suitcase and straighten things up. Then I'll get out as fast as I can. But the door doesn't have a snap lock. I'll have to climb back out the window! So give me plenty of time!"

Car lights showed through the trees, sweeping along the driveway. Jeff ran for the house like a startled giraffe and watched the car turn into the parking area and stop. By then, he was standing in the circle in front of the inn, trying to look as if he belonged there.

With a sinking feeling, he realized that if he had to describe the car, he would describe it as a flashy sedan. Furthermore, there were only two people in it, and one of them was fat. It was time to take steps. Jeff took them—straight toward the flashy sedan.

The driver struggled out and waddled around to open the door for his companion. The lights from the house showed only dimly on the parking area, but when the gentleman helped the lady out of the car, it looked as if her neck were on fire.

"I'll take this stuff down to my cottage and be right back," said the fat man. By then, Jeff was close.

"Good evening, sir," he said, and watched two

hundred pounds of lard almost jump out of a large skin. The lady took it a bit more calmly.

"Oh!" she said in a high, crackly voice. "You scared me!"

"I'm sorry, ma'am—"

"What are you doing, sneaking up on us?" snarled the fat man, breathing hard.

"I didn't mean to, sir. I'm sorry. I'm Jeff Adams, Mr. Bunker's new summer helper," he said, and turned to the lady. "You must be Mrs. Walling."

"That's right, and this is Mr. Wolfe."

"How do you do, Mr. Wolfe?"

Wolfe's answer was an irritable grunt. He opened the rear door of the car. "Grab that carton!" he ordered impatiently.

"Yes, sir! If you'll give me your key, I'll be glad to put this in your cottage for you," said Jeff eagerly.

"No, I'll go with you. I'll be right back, Myra."

"Take your time, Gus."

Mrs. Walling walked away toward the house on wildly high heels.

"That's a case of champagne," snapped Wolfe, "so don't slosh it around!"

Being as careful—and as slow—as he could, Jeff eased the heavy box out of the car.

"Come on, hurry up, I have to go to the can! That scare you gave me was nearly fatal!"

"Oh! Yes, sir!"

Jeff followed as Wolfe began to hotfoot it toward

his cottage. By now, Jeff's heart was in his mouth. How could he be sure Mr. Bunker was out of the cottage? What if something had held him up? It was time for desperate measures. There was only one way Jeff could think of to stop Wolfe. He would pretend to stumble and drop the carton.

He was getting up his nerve when from ahead of them came a strange, sinister sound. A sort of ripping noise.

Jeff put down his load and threw out a warning arm.

"Hold it!"

"What was that?" cried Wolfe.

"That's a skunk! An angry skunk sometimes makes a sound just like that. Stand absolutely still and let me take a look."

"Go ahead!"

Wolfe sounded scared stiff. Probably he was worried about his expensive, well-tailored clothes. He did not want to have to take them off and bury them. And one thing was certain, *something* was stirring in the grass around the corner.

Carefully Jeff tiptoed ahead and peered around the side of the cottage. Something was just disappearing around the other corner, but it was a little large for a skunk.

Jeff relaxed.

Then tensed up again.

The window screen was still pushed up!

Glancing back, he held up his hand, which was all the warning Wolfe needed. He stayed put. Jeff slipped around the corner out of sight and reached for the screen.

"Go on, beat it! Get away from here!" he shouted to cover the sound as he eased down the screen. This done, he returned and signaled Wolfe.

"All clear, sir. He took off."

"You're sure?"

"Yes, sir. I saw him go."

Wolfe followed Jeff timidly, hurrying along the side of the cottage and around to the door. While he was unlocking it, Jeff went back for the carton. Lights snapped on, the screen door slammed. When Jeff came in, he asked,

"Where shall I put the champagne, sir?"

"Leave it on the table," Wolfe called from the bathroom.

"Yes, sir."

Jeff set the carton down and left. He hurried through the dark toward the inn, walking along a path between the cottages. Pulling out his handkerchief, he wiped beads of sweat from his brow. Now he knew how Mr. Bunker felt.

A new sound startled him.

"Psst!"

He stopped.

"Jeff!"

He saw a dark plump form in the bushes.

"Sir?"

"I ripped my pants climbing out the window!"

"Oh! Was that the noise we heard?"

"Yes! You'll have to go in and sneak another pair out to me. I— Oh, good Lord!" Mr. Bunker clapped a hand to his forehead. "I left the screen up!"

"I pulled it down."

"Ah!" said Mr. Bunker gratefully.

Quickly he explained where his room was on the second floor. He described a pair of gray slacks hanging in the closet. Jeff glanced up at the second-floor windows.

"If you'll move over under your window, I'll drop them down to you."

"Good thinking!"

4

❖•❖•❖•❖•❖•❖•❖•❖•❖•❖•❖•❖•❖

When Jeff walked in, Mrs. Walling was standing behind the bar fixing drinks. Sparkles certainly lived up to its advance notices. Jeff had never seen such big diamonds with so much glitter.

Mrs. Walling's face was long and horsey, but her complexion was smooth, her flaming red hair looked like the real thing, and the sparkle in her blue eyes competed with her necklace, which was no small achievement. She looked up when Jeff came in, and a bright, off-center smile added still more sparkle to her appearance.

"Well! Is the champagne safe and sound?"

"Yes, ma'am."

"Where's Mr. Bunker?"

A good question.

"I believe he's outside looking for Ruby—"

As if she had been waiting to hear her name, Ruby barked and scratched on the door. Jeff turned and gave her a look that should have hurt her feelings.

"Oh, you bad girl," said Mrs. Walling, "you sneaked around him, as usual. Let her in and then find Mr. Bunker and tell him she's here, will you, Jeff?"

"Yes, ma'am."

Ruby waddled in, wagging her stubby tail, and if dogs can laugh she was laughing at Jeff as he rushed outside.

"Mr. Bunker!" he called loudly and scurried around the side of the house to where his boss was waiting. They spoke in whispers.

"What are you doing out here, Jeff? Where're my slacks?"

Jeff explained. Mr. Bunker gnashed his teeth.

"That devil dog! She *would* show up at the wrong time! Well, if Myra's in the lounge . . . listen, go around to the front door and up the front stairs! I don't know why I didn't think of that in the first place—nobody ever uses the front door. So go that way—but quietly!"

Leaving Mr. Bunker in his bush, Jeff circled around to the front of the house. Keeping his head low, he slipped inside and up the narrow front stairs like a cat burglar. A minute later, he was in Mr. Bunker's room rolling up a pair of gray slacks that were obviously the right size around the middle. He stepped to the window, slid the screen up quietly, and peered down. Below him he could see what looked like a small pale moon in the bushes. Mr. Bunker's bald head. Jeff dropped the slacks right on target.

"Ow!"

The slacks' belt had a huge steel buckle. Being heavy, it reached Mr. Bunker's head first.

"Hey!" Another voice was heard in the dark. "Who's that?"

It was Wolfe's voice, sounding alarmed again. He was in the driveway, walking toward the inn, and now he had stopped. Jeff stuck his head out the window and yelled down at the ground.

"Hey, get away! Beat it, you little stinker!"

Then he pretended to notice Wolfe.

"Oh—Mr. Wolfe! Watch out, it's that skunk again! Now he's over here! Come on, you stupid animal, take off!"

"Oh, for— What is this place, anyway, Skunk Hollow?" Wolfe asked angrily, but he turned and headed hastily for indoor safety. Jeff quickly checked Mr. Bunker's bathroom medicine chest, then rushed downstairs and back to the bushes. He found Mr. Bunker pulling up the gray slacks with one hand and holding a handkerchief on top of his bald head with the other.

"Now you've drawn blood! If I didn't need you,

I'd fire you! I tell you, with you around, I hope my Blue Cross is paid up!"

"I'm sorry! Here—I brought your styptic pencil. Shall I use it on your head?"

Mr. Bunker glowered at him in the dark.

"You think of everything—almost," he snapped, but bent his head.

"Ooh, that's quite a dent!" said Jeff. "Not bleeding much, though. This ought to fix it. . . ."

"Ouch!"

"Ssh! Your skunk imitation was lousy, by the way. Only a city slicker like Wolfe would have fallen for it."

"I wasn't trying to imitate a—" began Mr. Bunker, but then he had to laugh. "Well, anyway, you scared him off. . . . Okay, okay, that ought to take care of my head. Let's go inside."

"I found Mr. Bunker," Jeff reported brightly as he opened the door for the patient. Mr. Bunker shook a finger at Ruby and tried not to glare at her. She had that smiling look—tongue lolling out like a yard of red flannel—that big bulldogs go in for.

"You naughty girl, where were you?"

Mrs. Walling and Wolfe had just sat down at the round table. Wolfe was breathing a little hard and looking grumpy.

"Ruby can outwit you every time, Ambrose, and you know it," said Mrs. Walling. "What happened to your head?"

25

The injured man fingered it gently.

"I didn't duck low enough under a branch. Just a scratch. How come you're back so soon? You must have swallowed your dinner whole!"

"No, we didn't have any. After all the stuff they served at the cocktail party, I couldn't have eaten another thing."

Wolfe looked as if he could have, but he didn't say so. Instead he said,

"What a night! Listen, Ambrose, can't you do anything about that skunk that's hanging around this place like he owns it? Twice tonight, I might have got mixed up with him if it hadn't been for Jeff here!"

Mrs. Walling looked surprised.

"Since when have you had a skunk problem, Ambrose?"

"Er—just recently, Myra. Don't worry, I'm sure he won't be bothering us again. Jeff says he knows how to get rid of skunks."

Testing me to see if I can keep a straight face, thought Jeff as he busied himself emptying ashtrays. Being able to keep a straight face was obviously important around a place like Westham Inn.

Wolfe sat bulging in an armchair, holding his drink on his large belly with one chunky fist. As his humor improved, he gave most of his attention to Mrs. Walling. He looked at her a good deal, and when he did, his eyes seemed to reflect Sparkles' sharp glitter. He probably wished he owned it—most people would have—but that didn't mean he was a professional jewel thief right out of one of Mr. Bunker's favorite mystery novels. Gradually Wolfe's pout smoothed away into a smiling expression. Without looking exactly jolly, he managed to seem good-natured and sociable.

"By the way, Ambrose," he said, "I ran into a good buy at that big liquor store in the shopping center. Tomorrow night at dinner, the champagne will be on me."

"Champagne? Well! We'll live it up." Mr. Bunker glanced at Jeff. "Well, come on, Jeff, you might as well get settled. Grab your bag. I'll show you where your room is. It's out in the barn."

"In the hayloft," said Mrs. Walling.

"It is not. It's a darn nice room, as you'll see."

"Watch out for the field mice!" Mrs. Walling obviously loved to tease.

The barn was nearby. It was small and in good condition. Half of it was used for storage. The other half had been made into a plain but comfortable bedroom and bathroom.

"Looks fine, sir."

They shut the door, and Jeff immediately spoke in the sort of low voice suitable for private eye monkey business.

"Did you find out anything, Mr. Bunker?"

"About what? Oh! So much has gone on since I climbed out that cursed window, I almost forgot. . . . Well, no, not much. I wish I'd had more time. Darn the luck! I know the hostess of that party they went to, and she always serves too much food! Still, there *were* a couple of interesting things. First of all, his clothes."

"You looked at the labels?"

"Yes. No Chicago. Los Angeles, all of them. Of course, that could be explained, if he goes to the Coast a lot, but . . . One monogrammed handkerchief, but a *W,* so that's no help. The most interesting thing I found was a packet of business cards— AUGUSTUS V. WOLFE—and under his name, *Appraisals.* A Chicago post office box number, no other address."

"Appraisals?"

"Yes. Someone who goes around appraising estates. An appraiser looks at everything in a house and decides how much each thing is worth."

"But he said he was in the furniture business and had retired."

"Well, appraisals could be a part-time business he fools with—and he could also be a phony who uses the cards to get in places. Who knows?"

"If he's really an appraiser, he'd have to know the value of things. . . ."

"Right. Such as jewels."

"Such as jewels," Jeff agreed solemnly, playing

along—but at the same time he was beginning to worry. Once again, Mr. Bunker was showing Great Detective tendencies. He was sitting back, putting his fingers together, and narrowing his eyes. Something had to be done about it.

"If only Myra had left Sparkles at home in a nice comfortable safe-deposit box!" groaned Mr. Bunker.

"Well, I don't suppose she'll be wearing it all the time."

"Of course not. But it's almost worse when she's *not* wearing it! When she has it on, I at least know where it is! Well, get settled in and have a good night's sleep. If my head has healed by morning, we'll talk money." Mr. Bunker patted his wound gingerly. His bald head's splendid glitter almost rivaled Sparkles'. "What a night! Wolfe should complain! I've tripped over a wicket and flopped on the lawn, lost the cottage key, and been jumped by a wise guy. I've almost been caught climbing out a guest's window, ripped my best plaid slacks doing it, and been conked on the head. I'm aching in every muscle, and I've been called a skunk twice!—not to mention a little stinker and a stupid animal."

Jeff saw his opening and took it. He leaned forward earnestly.

"You're right, sir. You've been through a lot, and I hope we won't have another night like this. We were lucky this time, but the next time could be dif-

29

ferent. You could end up in the slammer for being caught with your hands in your guests' suitcases. And I'd hate to try to run this place while you were gone, because I just haven't had enough experience yet."

Mr. Bunker's eyes rolled, and he sighed.

"Jeff, with you around, it's going to be a long summer. Good night—I'm going to bed!"

5

◇•◇•◇•◇•◇•◇•◇•◇•◇•◇•◇•◇•◇

When Jeff showed up next morning, shortly after six, his boss was already in the kitchen. While they had a cup of coffee, Mr. Bunker explained Jeff's job.

"When things really get started, I've got two women who come in and clean; I've got several local girls who wait table; I've got a bartender—but if someone doesn't show up, you may find yourself cleaning a cottage or waiting table or doing almost anything except bartending. You're underage for that. You'll also mow lawns and do odd jobs. Today I'd like you to mow and trim the back lawn after breakfast is out of the way. And this evening—well, right now, with only two guests, I do the cooking myself, and— Can you wait table?"

"Sure. I've done a lot of that."

"Good. We'll be three for dinner, and you can wait on us. That'll save me some jumping up and down."

Something passing by the windows caught Jeff's eye.

"Speaking of jumping up and down, look at that!"

Ruby had romped into sight on the lawn, shaking a pair of badly torn plaid slacks over her head.

"I forgot!" cried her master. "I left those under the bush!"

They hurried outside.

"Ruby!" he called sternly, but in a low voice, so as not to wake the guests. "Drop those! Drop them at once!"

But Ruby had not been to obedience school, and she loved a good game. They ran after her, and all at once Mr. Bunker did another belly flop on the lawn. Ruby was so surprised she stopped to look. Jeff snatched the slacks away from her.

"That same fool wicket!" complained Mr. Bunker. "It got me again!"

"Hold it, sir! Hold the position. Now, let's see. If you had Mr. Wolfe's key in your hand, it ought to fly in this direction. . . ."

Jeff found the key.

At breakfast, Wolfe looked rested as he ate four fried eggs and half a pound of bacon. Mrs. Walling had black coffee and two pieces of dry toast and three cigarettes in a long ivory holder.

She was, of course, not wearing Sparkles at that hour. In some ways, she looked better when it was not around to compete with her snapping blue eyes. She laughed and joked and teased Mr. Bunker about everything, and got the same treatment from him.

"Ambrose, what kind of hamburgers are you going to give us tonight with our champagne?"

"Hamburgers? Do you know what a pound of hamburger costs today? You're getting chicken franks."

"And our wine in jelly glasses, no doubt."

"I have a chipped one just for you."

"The same one as last year? Oh, well . . . Say, what about the Collins estate auction Friday, Ambrose? Is it going to be a good one?"

"How could it be otherwise? I'm doing the catering at the refreshment stand! In fact, Hadley Ransom ought to be showing up any minute, to talk about the setup we'll have."

"I read Hadley's flyer—he's the auctioneer, Gus —and it says there will be colonial furniture, silverware, jewelry, paintings, prints, a tractor lawnmower, an automatic dishwasher—"

"A country auction, eh?" said Wolfe. "I haven't been to one of those in years."

"Not exactly a country auction," said Mr. Bunker. "Colonel Collins stayed in Europe for several years after World War II, then came home and bought a big place on a back lane over in the village. Odd man, though. Practically a hermit. Nice house full of beautiful things, but he never asked anybody over. Then he suddenly died of a heart attack. He didn't leave a will, so everything goes to two sisters in Omaha, and they're auctioning off the whole works."

A station wagon came racing up the driveway.

"And if you want to know anything more about the auction, here's your chance, Myra," said Mr. Bunker. "Here comes Hadley."

The car slid to a stop, shooting gravel onto the lawn. The auctioneer blew into the house, tall, noisy, and important, a walking advertisement for his business.

"My first of the season and a fine one," he boasted, after he had been introduced to Wolfe. "Come over to my place tomorrow morning, and you'll see. These things are so special we're allowing two days before the sale for people to look at everything, to decide what they want to bid on."

He paused, then lowered his voice in a confidential way.

"In fact, I've just had an exciting phone call. The curator of the American wing of a Boston museum is coming down tomorrow to have a look. Jason Brown."

"Jason Brown?"

Wolfe's voice was sharp as he repeated the name. Then, just as quickly, he recovered himself and was smooth and smiling again.

"Yes. Do you know him?" asked Ransom.

"Well, I've certainly heard of him," said Wolfe. "I've read several articles by him—I've always been interested in early American stuff."

"Did he ask about anything in particular?" Mrs. Walling wondered.

"Yes—the furniture, silver, and pictures. And jewelry; but then, that's just a hobby with him. The important stuff is the furniture. There's a colonial cupboard he may have heard about—a real museum piece."

Jeff cleared the breakfast table, put the dishes in the dishwasher, and went out to begin his yard work. There was plenty of lawn to mow and trim, and plenty to think about while he worked. For the first time, he really began to wonder about Wolfe. He was an appraiser. He showed up just a few days before a big auction—but did the auction have anything to do with it? Why did he look startled when Ransom mentioned a man named Jason Brown—a famous museum curator whose hobby happened to be jewelry? Was there really something fishy about Wolfe? Jeff sighed. One thing was certain: From now on, there would be no holding the Great Detective!

6

◇•◇•◇•◇•◇•◇•◇•◇•◇•◇•◇•◇

There was lots of lawn to work on. The broad expanse stretched from the cottages to the edge of a steep slope overlooking a pond. From the far end of the lawn, Jeff could catch a glimpse of salt marshes and the sea. A brook ran from the pond down through the marshes past an old gristmill. Several sea gulls were circling over the brook. Jeff was enjoying the clean air and the sunshine when his boss appeared. Jeff stopped the tractor mower.

"How's it going, Jeff?"

"Fine, sir."

The Great Detective lowered his voice dramatically.

"I guess you noticed how Wolfe reacted when Ransom mentioned Jason Brown."

"I sure did, sir."

"And you heard what Ransom said about jewelry. I hope you realize now that I wasn't just building a case out of thin air when I— Now, I want you to mow all the way to the edge, but don't fall off." Mr. Bunker's voice suddenly got louder. Then he whispered, "Don't look now, he just came outside." Then back to the loud voice, "and be sure to run the mower under the bushes. I don't want any long grass left under them." Being very casual, he glanced around at Wolfe and waved. Wolfe raised his hand in an absentminded way and kept going toward his car.

"But come back to the house for a minute now, Jeff," Mr. Bunker added in the loud voice. "I want to show you something."

Jeff got off the mower and walked beside his boss, who was keeping track of Wolfe with sideways glances. He led the way around the back of the house to a station wagon with Westham Inn on its door.

"I want to know where he's going. If he sees us, I'll tell him I brought you along to do some shopping. But I hope he won't see us. Jump in!"

They heard Wolfe's car starting. When they could hear it purring down the drive, Mr. Bunker started his car and edged around the corner of the house. Wolfe was just turning into the road. By the time they reached the head of the drive, Wolfe had curved off to the left onto Herring Brook Road.

38

"He's heading for the village. We can lag back and keep out of sight for a while."

As they topped a ridge here and there, they caught glimpses of Wolfe's car ahead of them. Soon they were in the village, and Wolfe had pulled into a parking lot. Mr. Bunker swerved off the road alongside the post office.

"This is perfect. Now, this is where you come in."

"Me?"

"Yes, you. I want you to follow him."

"What? My gosh, sir, I'm not exactly someone who can get lost in a crowd—"

"I know. A beanpole is hardly the best shadow I can think of, but it beats driving past him in a car with Westham Inn written on it."

"But I can't tail him! I'd feel silly!"

"Shall I hire a short kid tomorrow and fire you?"

"I'll tail him," said Jeff.

"Don't worry about it! If he sees you, tell him I'm at the post office and that I sent you to the drugstore."

Wolfe had hauled his butterball body out of his car and was waddling up Main Street. He had not looked their way. Feeling silly, Jeff sauntered along behind him, trying to look as little like a beanpole as possible. He did not have to tail his man for long, however, because soon Wolfe stopped and squeezed himself inside an outdoor phone booth.

Jeff was startled. What was this? A phone call so private he didn't want to make it from the inn?

Wolfe was facing away from Jeff and was preoccupied with putting his call through. And because of his bulk, he had left the door ajar. Jeff had to make a quick decision. Maybe if he stayed close he would be able to hear something significant. The only trouble was, he couldn't just stand there; Wolfe might look around and see him.

On the other hand, he *could* stop and tie his shoe. Bending down, almost kneeling, he quickly untied a shoelace and began tying it again. It took him several tries to get it right, during which time three or four people bumped into him and one big guy nearly fell over him. People were making grouchy suggestions about getting out of the way, and the noise of Main Street traffic was making eavesdropping a difficult job. He caught only a phrase here and there.

". . . got it all figured out . . . not much time . . . down here and bring . . . put it on thick. . . . Okay, good-bye."

"Oops!" said a squealy voice. It belonged to a girl who bumped into Jeff and spilled ice-cold Coke down his back. "Oh, now I've lost half my drink! Well, you shouldn't be in the way!"

Worse yet, the girl wasn't even pretty. She flounced away, and Jeff straightened up quickly before Wolfe turned to struggle out of the booth. He greeted Wolfe with a glad cry.

"Gee, I *thought* that was you, Mr. Wolfe! I'm glad

to see you—Mr. Bunker's at the post office, and he sent me to the drugstore, but I don't know where it is. Can you help me?"

"Why, sure, Jeff." Everybody likes to give directions. Wolfe pointed the way to the drugstore and walked off without the slightest air of suspicion.

" '. . . got it all figured out . . . not much time . . . down here and bring . . . put it on thick. . . .' Well, it doesn't tell us much, Jeff, but I think it *does* tell us Mr. Augustus V. Wolfe is up to no good!"

As they drove back to the inn, Mr. Bunker glanced at Jeff and grunted approval.

"For someone anybody can see a mile away, like the Empire State Building, you're a pretty good operator."

Jeff was busy pulling his shirt away from his back.

"Maybe, but I could have brained that girl. Boy, was that cold! I mean, it really straightened me up!"

"All part of the game," said the Great Detective. "Well, we've got a suspicious character on our hands, but I swear I don't know what to do about it."

"Watch him," said Jeff.

"That's right. We'll just have to see."

"Are you going to say anything to Mrs. Walling about this?"

"No. I don't see how I can, until we really have something solid to go on—and then it may be too late! I just don't know what to do!"

Back at the inn, sitting out on the lawn, Myra Walling had news.

"I handled a reservation!"

"I'm ruined!" said Mr. Bunker.

"No, I did a splendid job. A Mr. Pierpont Tuttle called from Boston. I gave him the cottage next to Gus's, and he was delighted. He'll be down this afternoon."

Wolfe, who had got back ahead of them and was slouched comfortably in a garden chair, laughed scornfully.

"Pierpont Tuttle! Now, there's a name for you. Sounds like a real stuffed shirt."

"When did he call, Myra?"

"Just a couple of minutes ago."

After Wolfe had made his private phone call, in other words. Was it just a coincidence, or were the calls connected? And what did they have to do with Mrs. Walling's necklace? Jeff glanced at Mr. Bunker, seated now in a chair. He had put his fingers together and narrowed his eyes.

7

Mr. Pierpont Tuttle, a small man in a large car with a chauffeur at the wheel, showed up at four in the afternoon. Mr. Bunker and Jeff went out to greet him. As he stepped out of the limousine and stood blinking in the sunshine, the fussy, formal little man fitted perfectly Jeff's picture of a Boston banker or head of a law firm or someone equally rich and respectable. If it weren't for Wolfe, Jeff knew he would have taken Mr. Tuttle at face value. As it was, he couldn't be sure.

"Very pleasant. Very pleasant indeed. I think I shall like it here. Mr. Bunker? Oh, yes, Mrs. Walling mentioned you. How do you do?"

Jeff took his bag from the chauffeur and offered to carry the large leather briefcase Mr. Tuttle was holding.

"No, no, I am used to managing it myself," he said in a fussy way. He turned to the chauffeur. "Thank you, Hamilton, you may go. I'll phone when I want you. . . . Now, which is to be my cottage?"

Mr. Bunker led him to the cottage next to Wolfe's, Jeff following with his bag. Mr. Tuttle inspected the rooms with a quick, birdlike glance here and there.

"Yes, yes, this will do nicely. I am very much in need of a rest. Your inn has been highly recommended to me. At what time is dinner served?"

"At seven."

"Very good. I shall get myself settled and take a nap."

Jeff put the bag on a luggage rack and left Mr. Bunker showing their new guest where extra blankets were stored in case he needed them. Over in the circle, the chauffeur had the hood up on the limousine, checking something. He closed the hood, dusted his hands together, and then got in the driver's seat. And suddenly Jeff had an idea. He walked up beside the car window.

"Boy, what a set of wheels!" he said admiringly. "Must be a treat to drive! I didn't know *anybody* rented limos like this one."

"Well, not everybody does, sonny, but we're the best in the business."

"What's the name of your outfit, Mr. Hamilton— in case I ever have a lot of money?"

"Harrod's." Hamilton chuckled. "Make a note of it."

"I sure will," said Jeff to himself as the limousine oozed away down the drive. By then, Mr. Bunker was coming back from Mr. Tuttle's cottage.

"What were you talking to *him* about, Jeff?"

"I asked him which limo outfit he's with. It's Harrod's. But don't worry, I was all ready in case I got an answer like, 'What are you talking about, kid? I'm Mr. Tuttle's chauffeur, and this is his car!' If he had said that, I'd have pulled a starry-eyed hick act— 'Gosh almighty, I sure didn't know *anybody* owned a car like this here 'un with a reg'lar chauffeur to drive it nowadays!' "

"All right, all right. So! We've got another character in a rented car, and you figure he's got to be a phony, too. Is that it?"

"He called Hamilton 'Hamilton' in a tone of voice that made it sound like he was his own chauffeur."

"Oh, did he, now? Well, let me just tell you something, my boy, I know a phony when I see one, and Mr. Tuttle is no phony. In this business, you have to be a pret-ty good judge of character, you have to be able to size people up, and I'm here to tell you that little pipsqueak is exactly what he looks like—a rich little pipsqueak. After a while, you get so you can tell."

"Well, all *I* can say is, it's darn funny you keep getting these guys checking in ahead of the season when you don't expect anybody."

"The man's tired *now,* so what's he supposed to

46

do—wait two weeks till the season starts before he comes down for a rest? Good grief, you *are* stubborn!"

Jeff's frown suddenly dissolved, and a snicker took its place.

"Talk about the pot calling the kettle black," he muttered, and after glaring for an instant, Mr. Bunker had to snicker, too.

"Stop bugging me and get that lawn mowed!"

"Well, I decided I had to wear Sparkles tonight if we were going to have champagne," Mrs. Walling remarked when she came down that evening before dinner. Standing inconspicuously in the kitchen doorway, Jeff had a good view of Mr. Tuttle when he joined the other guests in the lounge and saw Sparkles for the first time. He blinked rapidly and took off his rimless glasses to wipe them with his handkerchief. Mr. Bunker stood up to greet him and introduce him to the other guests.

"I hope you'll tell Ambrose how efficiently I handled your reservation," said Mrs. Walling.

"By all means," said Mr. Tuttle. "Your handling was faultless, Mrs. Walling."

"That's hard to believe," said Mr. Bunker, "but I'll have to take your word for it. And now I'd like you to meet Augustus Wolfe."

"Pleased to know you, Mr. Tuttle."

"Mr. Wolfe," said Mr. Tuttle, and gave him a

brief handshake. They displayed no more than polite interest in each other, like strangers who wanted to be agreeable. Jeff watched carefully and could not find anything to be suspicious about.

Wolfe asked Mr. Tuttle what he did.

"I have investments in several firms," he replied in his dry, precise voice. "It keeps me rather busy. I plan to retire soon."

He sat down with Wolfe and Mrs. Walling at a table in the lounge and asked for a glass of dry sherry. Mrs. Walling turned the conversation to the Collins auction.

"You're just in time for it, Mr. Tuttle," she told him.

Mr. Tuttle cleared his throat and looked doubtful.

"I—er—I'm not sure I approve of auctions. People tend to buy things they don't really need. . . ."

"Still, you shouldn't miss the fun." Myra Walling's blue eyes added their sparkle to Sparkles' sparkle. "And I'm sure you're a man of much too strong character to bid on anything you don't need. At any rate, tomorrow morning we can all take a look at what's going to be sold and decide what we don't need."

Mr. Tuttle's thin lips curled into a small smile, and he yielded.

"Well, I suppose there's no harm in looking. Perhaps I *will* go along."

"That's the spirit!"

49

8

⬦•⬦•⬦•⬦•⬦•⬦•⬦•⬦•⬦•⬦•⬦

Dinner was a great success. Even Mr. Tuttle allowed himself a glass of Wolfe's champagne. While Jeff was clearing the table before serving dessert, the phone rang. Mr. Bunker answered it in the kitchen just as Jeff came in with dishes.

"Call for Mr. Tuttle, Jeff. Tell him it's a Mr. Farwell and show him where the phone is in the small parlor."

Jeff delivered the message.

"Farwell! What does he want now?" Mr. Tuttle snapped impatiently as he rose from the table.

"I'll show you where you can take the call, sir."

The little man followed him to a small front room where Jeff pointed out the phone. As Mr. Tuttle picked up the receiver, Jeff kept going, out another

50

door that opened into the front entryway. He closed the door, but stayed within hearing distance.

"Yes, Farwell? What? Tomorrow? At what time? One o'clock? Oh, drat!" Mr. Tuttle sounded more annoyed than ever. "Is a meeting absolutely necessary at this time? If you ask me, Weatherby is getting to be an old woman about these things. . . . Well, if we must, we must, I suppose. Very well. Tell them I shall be there."

The instant he heard Mr. Tuttle hang up, Jeff did a fast tiptoe up the stairs and along the second-floor hall, then came down the back stairs and into the dining room by the time Mr. Tuttle had returned. Jeff resumed clearing the table without missing any of the conversation.

"Just when I hoped for a good rest!" fumed Mr. Tuttle as he sat down.

"Trouble?" asked Wolfe.

"Oh, I have to go back to Boston tomorrow for a one o'clock meeting. What a nuisance! I *knew* I should have kept Hamilton here! Now I must try to reach him."

"You mean, your chauffeur?"

"He's not my chauffeur. I merely rent a car when I want one," said Mr. Tuttle. "Heavens, I wouldn't think of bothering with the upkeep of a huge car and a chauffeur for the few times I need them! I simply use Harrod's, an excellent agency."

"The best," agreed Mr. Bunker, his eyes flicking

51

Jeff's way as Jeff headed for the kitchen with plates and silverware. Once there, he put the plates down very carefully and without any clatter so that he could continue to hear what was said.

"Well, now, listen, that sounds like an awful nuisance," said Wolfe. "Tell you what. Let's all take in the auction exhibit in the morning. Then if Myra will come along, I'll run you up to Boston."

He turned to her jovially.

"How about it, Myra? If you will, I'll take you to lunch at the best French restaurant in town!"

"Now, that sounds peachy," she said, her eyes dancing. "I'd love to go."

"Well, I must say, that's kind of you, Mr. Wolfe," said Mr. Tuttle. "You are sure it will be convenient?"

"Good excuse for a spree!"

Jeff had finished filling the dishwasher after dinner when Mr. Bunker came out to the kitchen and said, "I'll take care of the rest, Jeff. You can call it a night."

He also waggled his eyebrows meaningfully.

"Yes, sir," said Jeff. He left through the back door of the kitchen and went to his room in the barn. He had not been there long before he heard his boss outside calling Ruby. Then there was a tap on the door. He opened it. Mr. Bunker slipped inside. He sat down on a straight chair, looking pleased with himself.

"Well, Jeff, I hope you learned something to-night. Only a very rich man would talk the way Mr. Tuttle did about not wasting money on a car he didn't need. You can always depend on the very rich for one thing—they're very stingy. You wait and see —you'll get a dinky tip from *that* one."

Jeff glowered at his boss. He wished he could drop another belt buckle on his head.

"Okay, okay—but how about that phone call?"

"What about it?"

"Did you listen in?"

"Of course!"

"I only heard Mr. Tuttle's side of the conversation."

"I figured you'd manage that," said his boss with a sharp grin.

"How did Mr. Farwell sound?"

"Just the way he should. Like some junior member of the firm who has to notify the boss of something unpleasant."

"We junior members get all the dirty work."

"Who says you're a junior member? Their conversation was perfectly—"

A bump at the door made them both jump. It was followed by a whine.

"Oh, for—" Mr. Bunker sprang up and opened the door. "Ruby, stop that! If I really wanted you, you wouldn't come for fifteen minutes! And couldn't you just scratch on the door? Do you have to butt it down?"

Ruby romped in and attacked both of them, licking them affectionately. She had already decided that Jeff was her kind of guy whether he liked it or not.

"Down! Sit!" ordered her master, and after a moment, when she ran out of breath, she did. They got back to business.

"Well, *I* certainly wouldn't feel good about letting Mrs. Walling go off with those two crooks!" said Jeff.

"Crooks? Now, listen, don't lump them together that way!"

"Will she wear Sparkles?"

"No. Not for lunch, not even in a French restaurant. But don't think I've forgotten about Wolfe," said the Great Detective, going into the fingers-and-eyes routine. "I'm well aware that he might be up to something. Maybe he thinks he has a chance to grab Sparkles and use this excuse to get to Boston, so that he can stash it somewhere up there. Don't you worry! Before they leave, I'm going to have a word with Myra and make sure of Sparkles' whereabouts!"

9

"I want to see the Collins stuff myself," said Mr. Bunker next morning, when the guests were at breakfast. "Jeff, you can come, too. When the auction is on, you and I won't have much chance to watch. We'll be busy at the refreshment stand."

"You shouldn't have Jeff help you sell that stuff," said Mrs. Walling. "He's too young to start on a life of crime."

"Just for that, you won't get a mouthful," said Mr. Bunker.

"Think it's going to rain, Ambrose?" asked Wolfe. The sky was gray and gloomy.

"It might, but I doubt it. Not soon, anyway."

"It feels like rain to me," said Mr. Tuttle. "At any rate, I shall certainly take along my raincoat. Better safe than sorry, I always say."

Before long, they were all in the big tent behind Hadley Ransom's huge Victorian house. The tent was decorated with colorful pennants. It looked large enough to hold a circus. All the side flaps were rolled up to let in air and light.

When the auction was on, the tent would hold rows of chairs for the public. Now it was filled with pieces of furniture, household equipment, rolled-up rugs, and long tables on which smaller articles were displayed.

Mr. Bunker was nervous about Mrs. Walling. She was not wearing Sparkles, but—

"That crazy woman has it in her handbag, I'll bet you anything. I'm *sure* she has," he growled under his breath. "Keep an eye on her, Jeff. How do we know Wolfe hasn't hired a professional purse snatcher to be here?"

"Mr. Tuttle, maybe?"

Mr. Bunker moaned and slowly shook his head.

"Mr. Tuttle, a *purse snatcher*? Are you out of your mind? Please! Just concentrate on keeping an eye on Mrs. Walling, will you?"

"Okay, Chief!"

Jeff was able to watch her and still look at all the things that were going to be sold. He was amazed at how many different articles were displayed. He looked at the colonial cupboard that Hadley Ransom had said was good enough to be in a museum. He looked at tables, chairs, vases, pictures, glassware, fishing rods, and books. He saw an old-style phonograph that looked as if *it* ought to be in a museum.

Half a dozen old prints, behind glass in small frames, were hung on a free-standing panel. He had heard someone tell someone else they were good reproductions of Rembrandt etchings, but not worth bidding very much on. When Jeff stooped a little, their glass gave him a perfect reflection of Mrs. Walling across the tent. For a while he concentrated on the pictures, studying them one by one, and kept an eye on her at the same time.

The tent was crowded with people, many of them summer people who came early to their own houses. Hadley Ransom was moving about the tent greeting everybody. He was pleased to see so many prospective customers showing up.

"It will be too bad if it rains," said Jeff.

"Not at all," said the auctioneer. "Sunshine keeps folks out-of-doors."

Mr. Bunker had been making a round of the tent. He joined them now. Ransom beamed at him.

"Lots of interest in this auction, Ambrose. You'll sell a ton of food."

"I hope so, Hadley. By the way, when will that museum man be showing up?"

"Jason Brown? Late this afternoon, I hope."

"I'd like to meet him."

"Come back. I'll be glad to introduce you. Excuse me, there's Mrs. Frothingham! She buys everything!" Ransom rushed over to escort a large woman into the tent. Mr. Bunker and Jeff moved away through the crowd.

"I want to take a look at the refreshment stand setup, Jeff. You stay here and keep an eye on things."

Jeff was admiring an old Civil War rifle when a loud crash made him jump. It also made everyone else in the crowd jump and turn to see what had happened. The crash came from near the front of the tent. Like everyone else, Jeff moved in that direction.

Wolfe was standing by one of the tables looking embarrassed. An ugly, old-fashioned umbrella stand made of shiny brown-colored pottery had toppled over onto a box of dishes, and everything was smashed to pieces.

"I'm sorry, Mr. Ransom. It's my fault. I'm terribly clumsy," Wolfe was saying. "I knocked that stand over with my elbow. I'll be glad to pay for it and the dishes."

Hadley Ransom inspected the damage.

"You made a good choice, Mr. Wolfe—the umbrella stand was worth very little, and the dishes were just an odd lot of kitchen stuff. Don't worry about it."

But Wolfe insisted on paying for them. While this was going on, Jeff suddenly remembered Mrs. Wall-

ing. She was not there with Wolfe. He caught his breath and looked around wildly. What a chance for a purse snatcher!

At that moment, she came strolling through the crowd and joined Wolfe.

"Gus, was that you making all that racket?"

Jeff breathed again, but without complete conviction. He was glad to see she still had her purse—but did that prove Sparkles was still in it? What if some nimble-fingered pickpocket had recognized his golden opportunity?

Pink in the face, Wolfe answered her question.

"Yes, that was me—a bull in a china shop. I knocked over that umbrella stand."

Myra Walling inspected the wreckage.

"Well, you showed very good taste!"

Everyone nearby laughed except Jeff. He was too busy worrying. It was funny that Wolfe had been the one to knock over the stand. What if Mr. Tuttle just happened to be an expert pickpocket, and what if Wolfe had made that commotion on purpose, just to give him a chance to . . .

Mr. Tuttle!

Jeff looked around again more anxiously than ever, but in vain.

Where was Mr. Tuttle?

10

Craning his neck over the crowd, Jeff still saw no sign of Mr. Tuttle. He decided to find his boss in a hurry. Luckily, when he slipped outside, Mr. Bunker was already on his way back to the tent.

"What was all that racket?"

Jeff told him.

"And Mr. Tuttle's gone," he added. "Wolfe got everyone's attention, and now Mr. Tuttle's gone."

"Mr. Tuttle! Will you stop going on about Mr. Tuttle?" his boss demanded impatiently. But he suddenly looked more anxious than ever. "However, it *was* an opportunity for *someone* to get to work . . ."

"I wanted to go straight to Mrs. Walling and ask her if her necklace was safe, but I couldn't very well do that, especially with Wolfe standing beside her."

"No, you couldn't, Jeff—but *I'm* going to! This is too much for my nerves. Come on—you talk to Wolfe and give me a chance to speak to her."

"What are you going to say?"

"Well . . . I'll just remind her it's dangerous in crowds when something happens to distract everyone's attention. Don't worry, I won't tip our hand about Wolfe."

Wolfe and Mrs. Walling were still together, looking at the colonial cupboard. Jeff stopped alongside Wolfe.

"Find anything you want to buy, sir?"

"Not so far, Jeff, but I bought an umbrella stand I *didn't* want," he said with a genial smile.

"I'm glad it wasn't something more expensive."

"So am I!"

Jeff talked to Wolfe for another moment until he saw his boss had left Mrs. Walling. Then he excused himself and drifted away toward Mr. Bunker, who seemed to be feeling better.

"She squeezed her bag and told me not to be silly. Sparkles was safe and sound."

"Good. I'm glad that was a false alarm. Funny about Mr. Tuttle, though. I wonder where he went?"

"I don't know, and I don't care, and if I hear one more word from you about Mr. Tuttle, I'll put you on a bus to Vermont!"

"My lips are sealed," said Jeff.

Hadley Ransom came along and asked Mr. Bunker a question about the soft-drink deliveries. They went off together to his office.

Jeff walked around pretending to look at things some more, still keeping an eye on Mrs. Walling. After a while, he was back at the prints. He glanced at them, looking for one he particularly liked, and watching the reflection of the crowd in the glass.

Suddenly he stood back and stared at the display. Something about it wasn't right. The row of prints was still a solid row, but something about them didn't seem the same. He looked at each one, and when he came to the end of the row, there was a picture hook with no picture hanging from it.

The pictures weren't in the same order anymore.

And one of the pictures was gone!

At first, Jeff wasn't particularly concerned. Maybe Hadley Ransom had taken it down for some reason. Besides, Jeff had heard they were not very valuable. All the same, he decided he had better check. He glanced at Mrs. Walling. She should be safe enough, now that Mr. Bunker had reminded her to be careful in a crowd.

He hurried over to the back door of the house and asked a woman in the kitchen where the office was. She pointed the way.

The office door was open. He could hear Ransom and Mr. Bunker talking as he approached.

"Can I come in?"

They peered out the door, and Mr. Bunker said, "Now what?"

Jeff told them about the missing print.

"Did you take it down, Mr. Ransom?"

"No."

"Well, it's gone."

"Are you sure?"

"Yes, sir. And whoever took it must have put the end picture in its place, because they're not in the same order they were, and the end hook is empty as if whoever took the picture didn't want it to be noticed."

"It does sound that way." The auctioneer looked more annoyed than concerned. "Now, who the devil would take that? Those are only reproductions—good ones, but not worth stealing."

"Well, when Mr. Wolfe knocked over that umbrella stand and everyone was watching him, anyone could have taken it. And if somebody was carrying something, say a raincoat, he could easily have hidden a small picture like that under the coat," Jeff went on, careful not to look Mr. Bunker's way.

He might not be looking at Mr. Bunker, but Mr. Bunker was looking at *him.* The innkeeper spoke in a threatening voice.

"Hadley, what's the phone number of the bus station?"

"I didn't mention anyone in particular!" cried Jeff. "*Lots* of people out there are carrying raincoats!"

"What the devil are you two talking about?" demanded Ransom.

He never found out. Thanks to the office's open window, they had no trouble hearing another crash and clatter. Again it came from the tent. Ransom sprang up and looked out.

"What was *that*? Let's go!"

All three of them barreled past the poor woman in the kitchen, scaring her half to death. When they reached the tent, they found Wolfe standing beside a tangle of folding chairs. They were part of a pile stacked in one corner of the tent. Once again, he was red in the face. Mrs. Walling was standing by, laughing heartily.

"Mr. Ransom, I promise to leave at once!" he said. "I've done it again. I bumped into these chairs. But at least I didn't do any damage this time."

"We're going back to the inn, Ambrose," said Myra. "I want to change my shoes before we leave for Boston. We'll be back in time for dinner."

Standing behind them, raincoat over his arm, prim expression on his face, was Mr. Tuttle. There was obviously nothing concealed under his raincoat.

After further apologies from Wolfe, the three headed for his car. Ransom eyed Jeff.

"I thought you said Mr. Tuttle was missing."

"He was!"

As for Mr. Bunker, he was looking at Jeff with a

smug, let-this-be-a-lesson-to-you expression that Jeff found almost unbearable.

"Hmm," said Hadley Ransom. "Well, let's see which print was taken."

Ransom led the way across the tent. He reached the pictures first and had a chance to scan them before glancing around at Jeff.

"Kid, are you sure you feel all right?"

Jeff took a quick look and got a heavy jolt.

All of the pictures were there!

11

◇·◇·◇·◇·◇·◇·◇·◇·◇·◇·◇·◇

"But I tell you it was *gone!* The picture was missing, and so was Mr. Tuttle!"

"Are you sure?"

At that point, to Jeff's great surprise and considerable satisfaction, his boss went to bat for him. Mr. Bunker sighed.

"Listen, Hadley, this kid is a stubborn pest, but he's no nut. If he says they were missing, they were missing. So—"

"And Mr. Wolfe knocked down those chairs!" Jeff pointed out. "Another distraction!"

"The same technique magicians use," Hadley remarked thoughtfully. "They pull our attention off in the wrong direction while they're doing their tricks."

"Mr. Bunker, you've got to admit this is all too much to be just coincidence! I say Mr. Tuttle took the picture down the first time and put it back the second time. Let me see . . . here!" Jeff pointed. "This is the one that was missing!"

Ransom stared at it, shook his head in a baffled way, and took it off its hook. He turned it over for a look at the back. Small nails, tapped into the frame and bent over sideways, held the back panel in place. Ransom's attitude suddenly changed.

"Hey! Look at this. These nails have been twisted around. Here's a fresh scratch." He pointed to a place where a nailhead had inscribed a semicircular raw mark in the old wood. "The back's been taken out of the frame and not long ago, either!"

"Then maybe something else was inside, behind the print!" said Jeff. "Mr. Tuttle could have carried it under his raincoat out to Wolfe's car and taken something out of it, right?"

"Let's go back to my office," said Ransom.

Once there, he quickly removed the back panel.

"Hmm. Nothing here, of course . . ."

He turned the frame around and around, examining it intently.

"Wait a minute . . ."

Opening a desk drawer, he took out a pair of tweezers. From one corner of the frame, he pulled loose a tiny ragged triangle of paper. He studied it through a magnifying glass.

69

When he glanced up, he was excited and alarmed.

"This looks like very old paper. It could be a corner of an old drawing or an etching—"

Ransom bounced the palm of his hand off his forehead.

"Jason Brown! One of the things he asked about was these prints. He said he noticed them listed in our catalog. He said he supposed I was sure they were only reproductions of Rembrandt's etchings. I said of course I was sure. And I *am* sure! After he called, I even took another look at them."

He turned the print right side up to show them.

"Look at this one. Among a lot of other things, anyone with half an eye can see that the paper it's printed on dates from around the turn of the century. But *this!*" he said, pointing to the scrap he had found, "this is something else!"

He glared at the print, thinking. Then his eyes lit up.

"And suppose Jason Brown suspected Colonel Collins had got hold of the real thing somewhere. Suppose Wolfe *knew* he had the original and knew he had hidden it behind one of the reproductions."

While he talked, Ransom grabbed the phone and dialed a number. In a moment, he had been put through to Jason Brown's office at the museum.

"This is Hadley Ransom, let me speak to— What?"

He clapped his hand over the receiver and told them the bad news.

"He left just minutes ago! He's already on his way down here. Hello? Well, now, listen, this is urgent. Is your boss coming down here because of a picture? I must know, because we've just had a picture stolen. Please! I know you wouldn't usually give away your boss's secrets, but this is different! Unless I'm sure, I can't do anything about it, and by the time he gets here, it will be too late. So unless you want him to waste his trip down here . . ."

That got results. For a few tense moments, Ransom listened breathlessly. He asked a question or two. His expression changed several times. First he looked amazed. Then shocked. Then angry. His hand was trembling when he put down the receiver.

"Jason Brown is after a Rembrandt etching that was last seen in a Dutch museum the Nazis looted in World War II! His assistant refused to say why he thought Colonel Collins might have had it, but . . ."

Ransom's voice sharpened with alarm.

"Listen, if those two crooks have laid their hands on that etching. . . . We've got to catch up with them before they leave the inn!"

Mr. Bunker snatched up the receiver and dialed. "I'll tell Myra to stall. . . . Nuts! Line's busy!" .

"Well, let's go, we can't wait!"

They nearly trampled each other getting out of the room. The woman in the kitchen looked popeyed as they charged through again. They leaped into Ransom's big station wagon, and he gunned it down the driveway. A few drops spattered the windshield.

"Rain!" Ransom fumbled at the door beside him, and all the door locks went down.

"Wrong button," he mumbled and pushed another. This time all the windows rolled up. "That's better!"

Now that they were tearing along at breakneck speed toward the inn, it finally occurred to Jeff to wonder what they were going to do when they got there. Apparently that was beginning to bother the others, too. Ransom slowed down a little. The patter of rain had stopped, so he rolled the windows down again.

"Ambrose, do you realize that if Jason Brown hadn't been coming down here, Wolfe would probably have pulled this off by himself as slick as a whistle? Somehow or other, he must have found out that Collins had the original—and where he'd hidden it. All he would have had to do was put in the highest bid for that print, and nobody would have been the wiser."

Ransom sighed.

"And even now, we can't prove he's a crook. We don't have one shred of hard evidence. I mean, we don't dare accuse him and Tuttle of anything. We could still be wrong about this whole business. Suppose we accuse them of taking that print and then

can't prove it? Why, they could sue the pants off us! We can't take a chance like that, Ambrose.''

"You're right. We've both got too much at stake. Anyway, why should we?''

"That's right, why should we? If there *is* a Rembrandt involved, and we get it back, it won't put a dime in our pockets.''

"We're just asking for trouble.''

"You bet we are!''

Jeff was disappointed. But not for long. Hadley Ransom smacked one big fist on the steering wheel.

"Well, I don't care—nobody is going to get away with stealing a Rembrandt at one of *my* auctions!''

"I'm with you! We've got to nail those bums, or I'll never sleep again!'' Mr. Bunker declared, and Jeff leaned back, smiling.

"For one thing, it begins to sound like a real dirty business,'' said Ransom. "If Colonel Collins had that etching, he must have swiped it. If the Nazis had it first, then how did he get it? How much does Jason Brown know, or suspect? Well, whatever the story is, that etching ought to go back where it belongs, probably to Holland. But instead, Wolfe will sell it to some sleazy private collector who doesn't ask questions. There are plenty of those! Listen, Ambrose, what about Myra?''

"Leave that to me, Hadley. But even if I stop her from going with them, that won't keep Wolfe and Tuttle from leaving. Tuttle! I can't *believe* he's just a

74

little crook! He's got to be an eccentric millionaire or something!"

"If only we could stall them until Jason Brown gets here!" said Ransom.

"But that would take at least another hour. How can we stall them for that long?"

They had nearly reached the inn. From a high point on the road, they could see the house.

"Look! There they are, getting in Wolfe's car right now!"

"Slow down, Hadley! No sense in making them suspicious."

In the meantime, forgotten in the backseat, Jeff had been thinking, too, and with no more success than the others. Even now, they didn't know for sure that Wolfe and Tuttle were crooks. They didn't know for sure there was an etching. But if Wolfe and Tuttle were able to leave now, they'd *never* know.

The perfect crime?

12

◈•◈•◈•◈•◈•◈•◈•◈•◈•◈•◈

Ransom turned into the drive. Mrs. Walling waved to them from the front seat of Wolfe's sedan as they stopped alongside.

"Well! What are you doing here?" she asked.

"I'm going to get rid of that heap of mine!" said Mr. Bunker. "It wouldn't start again. Can you hold it a minute, Gus? I've got a couple of letters I wish you'd mail in Boston for me."

"Certainly, Ambrose." Wolfe looked very relaxed behind the wheel. Mr. Tuttle was sitting in back. His briefcase was on the seat beside him. He had a prim, smug look on his face that annoyed Jeff tremendously. If ever he had seen two men who looked pleased with themselves, it was this pair. As he got out of the station wagon, he glanced again at the case. If there *was* an etching, it would fit into it very nicely.

Mr. Bunker hurried toward the house. While they waited, Wolfe said,

"We enjoyed your exhibition, Hadley. I look forward to attending the auction, and I promise to sit still and not break anything."

"What, and spoil all the fun?" said Mrs. Walling.

Mr. Bunker stuck his head out the door.

"Myra! Telephone. Long distance."

She clicked her tongue.

"Now, who could that be? I won't take a minute."

Wolfe remained smooth, but he stole a glance at his watch.

"Yes, do try not to be too long, Myra, if we're going to get Mr. Tuttle to his meeting comfortably."

Mrs. Walling disappeared into the house. Now, of course, Mr. Bunker would tell her enough about what was going on to keep her from leaving with Wolfe and Tuttle. Hadley Ransom parked his station wagon nearby, then returned and stood chatting easily with Wolfe about various items in the auction. A couple of minutes ticked by. Then Mrs. Walling came out, looking disappointed.

"Oh, Gus, I'm so sorry, you'll have to go on without me. That was my cousin Ethel. She wasn't supposed to show up till next week, but she's coming today. She'll never forgive me if I'm not here to greet her."

77

It was a reasonable story. Mrs. Walling acted her part very well. Wolfe groaned, rolled his eyes, and protested.

"But we can be back here by six at the latest, Myra!"

Still, was it Jeff's imagination or did Wolfe's protest sound just a tiny bit hollow? Was there a hint of relief showing through? And Mr. Tuttle? Didn't he look more smug than ever?

"No, I'm sorry, Gus, I just can't go. You don't know Ethel. She's—well, she's a relative, and I guess we all know what that means!"

"I don't think I'm going to like her," said Wolfe.

"Dear me," tut-tutted Tuttle. "I hate to make you drive me all the way to Boston now, Mr. Wolfe, although . . ."

Wolfe sighed ponderously.

"Not at all, Mr. Tuttle. I can't let you down now. I'll just have to eat lunch for two! Now, why don't you move up here with me, as long as Myra's not going?"

Jeff stepped forward and opened the rear door for Mr. Tuttle, who took his briefcase from the seat and stepped out.

This is it, thought Jeff. Don't get funny. Remember, this is no skin off your nose. Be smart, and keep out of the whole business. You could get in big trouble. Just because this old prune is looking like a little smart aleck who's pulled off a fast one is no reason you should let it bother you. . . .

78

But even as he was thinking these safe, sensible, practical thoughts, something was happening inside Jeff. He got mad.

"No you don't!" he shouted angrily.

And snatching the briefcase away from Mr. Tuttle, he started running!

Behind him, shouts filled the air. Mrs. Walling screamed happily, Mr. Tuttle screamed unhappily, and Wolfe sounded as if he were using a bullhorn.

Racing across the lawn, Jeff sped down the path toward the pond. He was already appalled at himself. *Now* what have I done? he was thinking. Maybe there *was* something in the briefcase, but how was he going to open it and find out? It had a very fancy lock on it, and his time was limited. Sooner or later, he would have to face a furious Wolfe and Tuttle and probably the police. For that matter, maybe there was nothing but business papers in the case. If so, he could end up in jail. So now he was a hunted man, with a very uncertain future.

Swerving off the path, he plunged into the woods that surrounded the pond. He kept going for quite a while until he could no longer hear shouts behind him. Then he sat down against a tree and stared at the briefcase.

Its lock really was impressive. Not the tin kind most briefcases have. He didn't know how to pick a lock, anyway, so that was out. To look inside, he would have to force the case open. But as it hap-

pened, Jeff never went anywhere without his trusty Swiss army knife. He could manage it.

But suddenly he had a severe attack of cold feet. After all, even if they had stolen an etching, it might not be in the briefcase. So why break into it? Even if he went to jail, he might get off easier if he had not broken into the case. Jeff groaned.

"You dummy, you've really done it this time!"

He saw himself in a striped suit—broad stripes, running horizontally. For a moment, he almost panicked. Then he remembered Jason Brown. The thing to do was to hide out until Brown had time to get there. That was his best chance.

Jeff got to his feet and began to slip through the woods, looking for a good place to hide. Minutes later, he was under a bush in the thickest patch of underbrush he could find. The woods were not as thick as he wished they were. He would have liked something more like Yellowstone Park. But at least he felt reasonably safe.

In no time at all, however, he heard the sound of feet crashing through the underbrush.

RAT-A-TAT-A-TAT!

At first, he thought he'd been machine-gunned. But then, when his heart started beating again and his eyes uncrossed, he saw that somebody was beating the underbrush directly over his head.

Jeff crawled forward and stared straight up into the startled eyes of a small middle-aged man in droopy khaki shorts with a whistle on a lanyard around his neck. Jeff sighed. He was not going to add assault and battery to the counts that were already piling up against him.

"Okay, I surrender," he said meekly.

Droopy Shorts goggled down at him.

"I beg your pardon?"

"I said, I surrender."

"You what?"

"Well, aren't you a—er—what are you, anyway?"

"Why, I'm a nature-study leader!"

"A what? I mean, you are?"

Droopy Shorts eyed him as if he suspected Jeff of being "armed and dangerous."

"I have a group of teenagers with me, and several of them outweigh you," he blustered, letting Jeff know he had him outnumbered and outmuscled.

Jeff laughed hoarsely. He struggled to his feet and picked up the briefcase.

"Gee, I thought you were one of *our* group! We're playing a chase game. I'm supposed to be carrying a briefcase full of Top Secret papers, and the rest are trying to track me down. Darn it, now you've probably spoiled our game!" he added crossly, building up his story as he went along. He walked away with as much evidence of indignation as he could muster, leaving Droopy Shorts with his mouth open, but at least not reaching for his whistle.

Jeff concentrated on putting as much distance as

he could between the nature-study group and himself. He hurried on through the woods and picked up a path, but quickly left it when he heard more voices. All around him, he could hear them and the tramp of feet through the underbrush. There had to be more than one group around; in fact the woods must be crawling with nature-study groups, he decided bitterly. Some group or other seemed to be straight ahead of him—but then, it could hardly be Droopy Shorts' gang, so why not get back on the path where he could make better time—just keep walking and act natural, as if he were merely out on a nature walk himself?

True, he probably looked a little odd, carrying a briefcase in the woods, but he would have to risk that. He would simply nod pleasantly and say hi and keep walking.

Two boys a little younger than he rounded a bend in the path ahead of him. Jeff did his pleasant-nod routine.

"Hi."

"Hi." The boys eyed him curiously, especially his briefcase. Jeff held it up and said cheerily, "My lunch!" as he went by. Behind him, the boys had stopped. He did not dare look back, but he was sure they had stopped to watch him. He walked on as fast as he could without actually breaking into a run.

Somewhere in the distance, a siren wailed. A police car, no doubt. Jeff started guiltily and almost stumbled. He hoped the boys had not noticed.

Once around a bend in the path and out of sight, he began to run. He rounded another bend.

A skinny twelve-year-old wearing enormous glasses sprang in front of him, his arms spread wide.

"Stop!"

13

Jeff's first impulse was to push the kid in the face and keep running.

Just in time, the boy spoke again.

"We're taking a picture! Hold it a minute, or he'll fly away!"

Jeff skidded to a halt.

"Who'll fly away?"

"The Great Spangled Fritillary!"

"The what?"

"The butterfly!"

Jeff peered past him. Crouched beside the path was another boy with a camera. He had it trained on a low bush. Glancing back nervously over his shoulder, Jeff fidgeted.

"Well, snap it up, I'm in a hurry!"

"You can't hurry nature photography. You gotta have patience. Just a minute . . . Okay, Eddie?"

"Naw, Buzzy, he won't open his wings!"

Jeff gritted his teeth.

"Open your wings, you stinker!"

The camera clicked.

"Got it!"

Buzzy was impressed.

"Say, you got the touch!" he told Jeff.

"Out of my way!" By now Jeff was up to *here* with nature lovers. And he was conscious of the fact that Buzzy and Eddie gave his briefcase a funny look as he went past. He thought terrible things about them and glared at the Great Spangled Fritillary as it fluttered frivolously away down the path ahead of him.

In the distance, he could hear sirens again. For a small resort town, Westham seemed to have plenty of cops!

He left the path for the woods. From now on, he would have to pit his skill as a woodsman against the world—and he was not much of a woodsman. Just living in a small town in Vermont didn't make you Daniel Boone. Jeff was never even quite sure which side of a tree the moss grew on.

Furthermore, he did not know the area he was in. He wished he had been at the inn a little longer, with a chance to take some walks so that he would know what sort of places were around the pond. Not far ahead, through the trees, he saw what looked like dense undergrowth. He headed that way and quickly got caught on some brambles.

"Ouch! Ouch! Ouch!" he muttered as he picked himself loose. Next he heard water running. A stream was somewhere nearby. In a moment, he found himself on the edge of a small brook. Small, but much too wide to jump across. Still, once across the brook and into the woods on the other side, he should be safe.

Jeff was trying to cross the brook on some slippery rocks when he saw an old mill downstream and realized what he had done.

"Oh, for Pete's sake!"

What he had managed to do was run all the way around the pond and get back almost to where he had started—the last place he wanted to be! He could even see a part of the road in front of the mill, and as he watched, a police car pulled up. The sight of it so unnerved him that he slipped off the rocks and wallowed around in water up to his knees. He almost dropped the briefcase.

Scrambling up the bank, he scurried back in the direction he had just come from, soggy slacks slapping his ankles and water squirting out of his shoes. From somewhere around him, he heard a sharp whistle. A police whistle, surely! They were closing in on him!

At that moment, desperation hardened him. Was he going to let himself be taken with the briefcase

87

without even knowing what was in it? After all, only one thing could save him now, and that was for a Rembrandt etching to be there.

He glanced around. All was peaceful. A bird chirped somewhere in the underbrush. Now was the time! He sat down in a small clearing and reached for his trusty Swiss army knife.

A whistle seemed to split his eardrums.

"Grab him, girls!" cried a familiar voice. The voice of Droopy Shorts. Girls of every size and shape seemed to spring out of the earth all around Jeff. He went down under a heap of them. What could he do? He couldn't hit girls. Not that it would have done any good, because he didn't have a chance. They might only be girls, but there were a whole lot of them, and some of them were pretty hefty. Another whistle sounded. Heavy feet pounded up.

"Officer, there's your man! Er—boy, that is!"

"Where?"

"Well, he's under there somewhere. Get up, girls, and let this officer take charge!"

14

◇•◇•◇•◇•◇•◇•◇•◇•◇•◇•◇

The officer was Constable Caleb Hodge of the Westham Police Department. He said so.

He stared grimly at Jeff.

"You Jeff Adams?"

"Yes!" said Jeff, and turned furiously on the nature-study leader. "You said teenagers!"

Droopy Shorts smiled smugly.

"Well, they *are* teenagers. Think I was going to tell you they were girls? I knew you were up to no good the minute I saw you!"

"I'll take charge of that there briefcase," said Constable Hodge. "He stole it."

"He did? Gee!" The girls found this very exciting.

"Come on, kid," said the constable. "I'm taking you back to the inn."

Constable Hodge marched Jeff downstream to a small bridge and up the other side of the brook. The whole nature-study group tagged along at their heels.

"We followed him, and when he turned back, we set a trap for him. He was no match for our woodsmanship!" their leader said proudly.

"Good work," said Constable Hodge. "Well, here's the path up to the inn. I'll take him from here."

The nature group let out a group groan.

"Can't we come, too?"

"No. This is official business. I'll handle it."

Jeff was glad to hear it. He looked back at his tormentors.

"You heard the man. Scat!" he said, and left them glowering at him, especially Droopy Shorts.

"Just keep walking up that path, sonny, and don't try to run away, if you don't want to get a leg shot off," the officer warned him sternly.

As they mounted the path, Jeff was in despair. Even if Jason Brown had arrived, would he be of any help now? They had nothing to go on but suspicions. They couldn't *make* Mr. Tuttle open his briefcase.

Jeff had gotten himself into real trouble, and all in vain. A rumble of thunder in the distance, grim and foreboding, fit right in with his mood.

When they reached the top and walked onto the

broad, level lawn, all the people Jeff had left behind were still there, and they all hurried his way. But he didn't see any strangers. No Jason Brown.

"Got him!" said the constable. Mr. Tuttle rushed forward and all but dragged the briefcase out of the officer's grasp.

"Thank you, Officer, thank you! There are important bank papers in this that would be dreadful to lose!"

As he talked, he was examining the case with an eagle eye.

"Well, thank heavens! It seems to be all right. Mr. Wolfe, I must leave at once!" The little man shot a hateful glance at Jeff. "I don't know what this young scoundrel thought he would gain by stealing this, but all he's accomplished is to make me late for my meeting!"

Mr. Bunker and Hadley Ransom and Mrs. Walling were all staring at Jeff speechlessly. They looked as if they wanted to help, but couldn't think of anything to do. Wolfe looked as if he knew what he would have liked to do, and it wouldn't have been pleasant.

Ruby came over and nuzzled Jeff's hand. He patted her head sadly—and suddenly thought of a final straw to grasp at.

"Wait a minute! That briefcase is evidence, isn't it, Officer?"

Constable Hodge reddened with annoyance,

looking as if he wished Jeff had not reminded him.

"Well . . ."

"Of course it is!" said Mrs. Walling.

"Oh, now, look here," Mr. Tuttle snapped impatiently, "since it's my case, and I've got it back, what does it matter? I'm not really interested in charging this boy with anything. I think what he really needs is a doctor!"

Jeff had talked his way out of jail. But now he was after more than that.

"No, sir," he said stubbornly. "I'm not going to have him claim later on that I took something out of that case. He's got to open it up right now and make sure everything is there!"

Constable Hodge stared at him.

"Boy, you *are* crazy! If this gentleman is satisfied and doesn't want to prefer charges against you, you better leave well enough alone!"

But now Mr. Bunker stepped forward. The expression on his round face was beautiful to behold. Full of understanding. He laid his hand on Jeff's shoulder.

"Now, hold on, Caleb. Jeff's right. Mr. Tuttle should check the contents of his bag right now, in front of you."

Mr. Tuttle drew himself up haughtily.

"I'll do nothing of the kind. The papers in this case are of an extremely confidential nature. I wouldn't think of showing them to *anyone*. Besides, it's perfectly obvious the case has not been opened."

"Maybe he picked the lock," suggested Hadley Ransom. "I could."

"Not this lock, Mr. Ransom," snapped Mr. Tuttle. "It's a very special lock."

"I could do it with my eyes shut. Here, let me show you—"

"Don't be ridiculous, Mr. Ransom! Now, really, I can't stand here arguing any longer. There are plenty of witnesses here, Constable, to testify that I hereby relinquish any right to claim later on that anything is missing from my briefcase."

"Sounds fair enough, sir," said the constable.

"And I can't thank you enough; in fact I certainly want you to have something for your trouble—for your police fund, that is," said Mr. Tuttle, and set the briefcase down beside him so that he could reach for his wallet.

Thunder went in for some more melodramatics, closer now, and a drop or two of rain spattered down.

Jeff looked around and did some fast thinking. He was in the clear again, off the hook. He should let well enough alone. But on the other hand . . . Tuttle was busy taking out money. Constable Hodge was busy watching him do it. Hadley Ransom's station wagon was fifty feet away in the parking area. Jeff measured the distance with a glance and thought, here we go again.

Stooping suddenly, he scooped up the briefcase and made a beeline for the station wagon.

Jeff was on his way before any of them moved. Then it was cries and confusion and everyone running behind him. Constable Hodge nearly grabbed him as he went by, but was taken out of play by an unexpected helper. For once, Ruby did the right thing—she grabbed the officer's trouser leg and sent him sprawling. It was Wolfe, surprisingly enough, who led the pack.

Jeff banged his head only a little diving into the front seat. He turned the ignition key so that the buttons would work. By the time Wolfe was within ten feet of the car, Jeff had pushed the door locks' button. By the time Wolfe reached the car, he could only bang on the windows, because Jeff had pushed the button that rolled them up.

"Get out of there! What are you doing? Stop that!"

Tuttle and a purple-faced Constable Hodge were not far behind, and all three watched in horror as Jeff's Swiss army knife's screwdriver pried ruthlessly and successfully at the case's lock. Thunder cracked, and all at once the heavens opened.

"Don't let him do that!" screamed Tuttle—but it was too late. Jeff had pulled out the papers inside,

and what was on top of them made his heart do cartwheels. He turned his find sideways so that all could see, and treasured the sight of Wolfe and Tuttle standing in the rain looking like two drowned rats.

15

♦•♦•♦•♦•♦•♦•♦•♦•♦•♦•♦

The museum curator took one look at the etching and began to act more like a small boy on Christmas morning than a dignified art expert. Jason Brown almost danced up and down.

"It's the Rembrandt! It *is* the Rembrandt!" He slapped Jeff on the shoulder. "Young man, the Dutch will make you a national hero!"

Once he had recovered himself, they all sat down in the lounge—all but Wolfe and Tuttle, who had left in the custody of a shocked Constable Hodge—and he told them his side of the story.

"After World War II, I was part of a special army group whose job was to search out and recover art treasures looted by the Nazis. Colonel Collins was the head of the group.

"We found everything that was missing from one

Dutch museum except for one especially important Rembrandt etching. Long afterward, I realized Collins might have had a chance to take it before we junior officers knew about it, and since I'd never felt he was a thoroughly trustworthy man, the thought stayed in my mind.

"When I received your catalog, Hadley, and learned he had died, I thought there might be a chance the etching was still in his possession. Not much of a chance, but worth coming down here for a good look at everything. Now, your guesses are as good as mine as to how Wolfe came to know where the etching was hidden. He probably intended simply to buy the reproduction at the auction, but when he heard I was coming he got nervous. So he decided to get his hands on the etching before I showed up. His plan with Tuttle was a dandy, and it would have worked if it hadn't been for this young man."

Jeff turned red and smiled at Mr. Bunker.

"I owe it all to the boss," he said. "If he hadn't been suspicious of Wolfe in the first place—"

"For the wrong reasons," admitted Mr. Bunker. "And if you ever mention Tuttle again, you're fired!"

Myra Walling laughed.

"Ambrose, you're my favorite idiot!"

She opened her purse and took out her diamond necklace. It flashed fire as she twirled it gently.

"And to think, it all started because Ambrose was

worried about Sparkles! You naughty thing, you've caused a lot of trouble."

Jeff glanced at his boss, chuckled, and said, "Yes, that's the trouble with diamonds."